Fatima

Has A Gift

By Dionne L. Grayson

Fatima Has A Gift: The Children's Gift Series
Copyright © 2021 Dionne L. Grayson
ISBN: 978-1-952327-39-1
Library of Congress Control Number: 2021902310

Printed in the USA
T.A.L.K. Publishing, LLC
5215 North Ironwood
Suite 200 J
Glendale, WI 53217
publishwithtalk.com

DEDICATION

To all the fathers, mothers, and guardians
who are raising children with gifts - You have the
awesome responsibility of cultivating what has
been placed inside each of them. I pray for
your understanding and wisdom as you help
propel them into what they were designed to do.
My hope is that this book will spark something
as you move forward with your child(ren) in
exploration, exposure, and guidance.
Let's look inside and see!

This Book BeLongs To:

_____

1

Fatima has a gift!
Let's look inside and see!

2

3

Fatima has a gift!
And it's for you and me!

4

5

Fatima has a gift!
It's what she loves to do!

7

Fatima has a gift!
I know that you do too!

Cut, sew, sketch, and style…

11

Models on catwalks make Fatima smile!

13

Fashion is Fatima's gift,
her gift for you and me!

Fatima's gift is for the world,
for all of us to see!

A costume designer or tailor
are careers that she can choose.

19

They all have Fatima's gift,
this really is good news!

If you love fashion like Fatima,
if it's what you love to do,
a costume designer or tailor
may be the career for you!

Costume Designer

A costume designer designs clothes and accessories for people to wear.

Tailor

A tailor is a person who makes
clothes fit a person perfectly.

Will you please help Fatima find what she needs to sew a dress?

1. Measuring tape
2. Red fabric
3. Purple fabric
4. Scissors
5. Sewing machine
6. Needle and thread

THE END

Made in the USA
Middletown, DE
29 October 2021

Fatima Has A Gift

As Fatima explores her gift with style and how it connects to fashion, children are introduced to purposeful careers with repetition, sight words, and vivid illustrations of characters who come to life on the pages!

The Children's Gift Series targets early level readers, ages 5 – 7, and can serve as read-aloud books for daycare ages. The series features 10 books that will help children explore their gifts and how they connect with a variety of careers.

About The Author

Dionne Grayson is the owner of Building Your Dreams, LLC., where she empowers youth and adults to live life By Design. Her signature program Dream.Explore.Build. partners with teens as they explore their interests and how those can connect to a career path full of purpose.

ISBN 978-1-952327-3
$14
514

9 781952 327391